The New LiBEARian

Alison Donald & Alex Willmore

For Alastair, Kenzie, Gemma and ... adventure! A.D. • For Dara, A.W

PLEASE KEEP THE LIBRARY TIDY

Watch Out for BEARS

BLAST OFF WITH BOOKS

A hush fell over the library.
Storytime was about to begin.

KIDS' CORNER

Dee wiggled
and wriggled
and jiggled.

"Is it time?" Dee asked.

Except....

"Miss Merryweather's not here," said Jack.

"Maybe she's late?" said Dee.

"She's never late," said Kenzie.

"Something's not right," said Dee. "Come on, let's find her!"

PLEASE KEEP THE LIBRARY TIDY

"Look! Footprints! A clue," said Dee.

"They're not grown up footprints," said Jack.

"They're not kid footprints," cried Alex.

"They're not footprints at all," said Dee.

The children ran through the bookshelves,
following the paw prints through a galaxy, into an ocean

and down a runway, only to find...

More clues!

"The desk feels sticky," said Jack.

101 RECIPES FOR HONEY

"And look," said Dee,
"the books are shredded and torn."

And then Dee found someone unexpected...

A new librarian!

"You're not our librarian.

Where's Miss Merryweather?" Dee asked.

The new librarian shrugged.

"Will you read us a story?"
The new librarian nodded.

"Oh, thank you!" cried Dee.
"We've been waiting for ages!"

"Could you read us a..."

"A princess story?"

"A pirate story?"

"A book about dragons?"

But the new librarian looked bored.

"How about something different?" Gemma suggested.

"Something exciting," said Jameson.

"Something we're not allowed to read," said Tom.

"Could you read us a scary story?" asked Dee.

The new librarian's ears perked up and he grabbed a truly scary book about...

Bears!

He opened the book and **ROARED!!!**

"**AHHH!**" the children screamed.

He **GROWLED**

and **STOMPED,**

and ROARED again.

BEAR

The children shivered and quivered.

"Read it again," they cried until…

"Someone's coming!" said Dee.

"Hello children, sorry I'm late," said Miss Merryweather, the usual librarian. "A volcano erupted in the ancient history section and there was hot lava everywhere! But it's all cleared up now."

"Okay, settle down. Today's story is:
Goldilocks and the Three Bears," she began.
"Ooh, we love bear stories!" Dee cried.

"Once upon a time there were three bears. Papa Bear, Mama Bear and Baby... Oh!"

"Where's Baby Bear?" the children cried.

"Baby Bear, I know you're hiding.

It's time to come out now," the librarian called.

The new librarian shuffled over sheepishly.
"Baby Bear, my dear, you're late for storytime too,"
said Miss Merryweather.

"Goodbye Baby Bear,"
the children cried as he
stepped back into his story.

"Now, let's start again,"
said Miss Merryweather.

"Once upon a time there
were three bears...

Except..."

"Where's Goldilocks?"

The End

The New LiBEARian
is an original concept by
© Alison Donald

Author: Alison Donald
Illustrator: Alex Willmore

Published by
MAVERICK ARTS PUBLISHING LTD
Studio 3A, City Business Centre, 6 Brighton Road,
Horsham, West Sussex, RH13 5BB
© Maverick Arts Publishing Limited
August 2016   +44 (0)1403 256941

A CIP catalogue record for this book
is available at the British Library.

ISBN 978-1-84886-223-4

let's ★ Read

www.maverickbooks.co.uk